This is a work of fiction. Names, characters, places, and incidents either are the product of the author's imagination or are used fictitiously, and any resemblance to actual persons, living or dead business establishments, events, or locals is entirely coincidental.

The scanning, uploading and distribution of this book via the internet or via any other means without permission of the publisher is illegal and punishable by law. Please purchase only authorized electronic or physical editions, and do not participate in or encourage electronic piracy of copyrighted materials. Your support of the author's rights is appreciated.

Published by: thedimosvault.com

Boston. 2018

ISBN-13: 978-1718796041

ISBN-10: 1718796048

I Echo

To Impact. For showing me God's love.

For letting me show it back to you.

Table of Contents

November 2nd 2015	2
December 9th 2015	13
February 3rd 2016	21
May 13th 2016	25
September 5th 2016	28
October 4th 2016	31
December 14th 2016	35
March 23rd 2017	37
July 14th 2017	41
July 23rd 2017	44

All my life, I have found Beauty in Everything,

except Myself.

November 2nd. 2015

The echoes of emptiness flooded over me.
You know what I'm talking about, right?
That feeling you sometimes get. The one that stretches on forever as it wraps itself around your chest like a vise that tightens with every breath. It's not there, not really, but you can still feel the weight of it. Reaching out, I picked up my phone from the bedside table and clicked it on. 1:30 A.M.
I tossed myself over in a mini fit of irritation. Why couldn't the weight just go away? It wasn't like I asked for it, why the hell was it even here?
Tossing over again, I let loose a jumble of frustrated noises.
Go to sleep, Cathy!
I curled my body up into a ball, hands cradling my head, waiting for darkness to replace the silence.

An awful ringing shattered my ears and threw me awake.
Breath quickening, I reached out from beneath the light blue comforter. Grabbing my phone, I swiped the alarm off before slumping back, tiredness assaulting my eyes like a headache that flickered in and out with every blink. The phone read 6:03 A.M.- fastest three minutes ever!
   Heaving a sigh, I pushed the blankets off of me, accepting the late fall cold air that washed over me with a series of groans and socially acceptable alternative curse words. From the rather large bean bag that sat in one corner of my room, I grabbed the outfit I had laid out the night before and marched out of my room and down the hall, towards the bathroom. Downstairs I could hear the murmur of voices. That was good. Turning on the shower, I shed my PJ's and tossed them into the laundry basket and stepped beneath the warm stream of water. It was probably going to be the calmest and quietest moment of the entire day.

After I was clean and dressed, my teeth brushed and hair put together, I stood in front of the mirror and studied myself intently, head tilted slightly to the left. I don't look right, was all I could think. Jeans and a red sweater clinging to my thin body, head framed by blond hair, it all seemed to cling to me. A quick glance at my phone told me the time was 6:45, no time to make myself look better, there was an hour-long bus ride waiting for me. Joy.

Opening the door let in a rush of cold air, and I hurried down the stairs, grabbing a sweatshirt off the coat rack by the door and pulling it on as I went. I could hear the little kitchen TV in the next room. Passing by the living room window, I saw that dad's car was gone, and I breathed a mini sigh of relief. Mom was in the kitchen humming quietly to herself.

"Morning," the words came out of my mouth a little too brightly.

I watched my mom's eyes widen in surprise. Apparently, she hadn't heard me come down the stairs.

"Hey sweetie," she gave me a smile and a kiss on the forehead.

"Ready for school?"

I shrugged.

Not as though I got to stay home if I wasn't ready. Grabbing my lunchbox off the counter, I wandered back into the living room where my backpack waited.

"Ready as ever, gotta go, if I'm gonna make the bus. See you later ma, love you!"

I called the words over my shoulder as I exited and headed down the street to where the bus stop was, a group of neighborhood kids bunched up around it, talking and laughing to each other.

My phone vibrated in my hand. Thumbing it on a smile crept across my face at the name that flashed on the screen. Abby always finds a way to make me smile, the crazy soap opera that is her life helps me forget mine for at least a little while most of the time.

We neeeed to hang out this weekend!!!!!

I circled my way around the crowd of neighborhood kids and leaned against the fence that separated one of the many houses from the sidewalk.

Don't know if the parents will go for it, but I'll ask.
They never let you do anything since you moved ☹

You're telling me, mom's always working and dad only wants to stay at home and work on his scripts.

Like he's going to be the next big thing. Honestly, I'm not even that far away.

Yeah, I know, still more effort than me just walking two houses down though.

Yeah ☹

Off in the distance, I could hear the bus, and looking up I caught sight of it stopping at the stop sign before turning right onto our one big loop of a street. Shouldering my bag, I tucked my phone back into my back pocket and got in line with everyone else, the sun warming my face but just slightly. When I was securely seated as far back in the bus as I could go, the sea of unfamiliar faces now just one of hats and the back of people's heads, I pulled my phone out once more. The bus peeled away from the curve, and the world exploded with noise. It was going to be a long day.

I could tell you all about the day and just how long it was, but I don't really remember it. Back on that same bus many hours later, all I knew was that I had a lot of homework and that everyone in my math class thought I was an absolute know-it-all. I don't know why it bothered me so much, but it did, and the more I thought about it, the more my chest seemed to tighten...

I pushed the thoughts aside, for once. It was too early for the vise. Maybe if I avoided it now, I wouldn't have to deal with it later. That was a concept. As if moving hadn't been frustrating enough, I still hadn't made any actual new friends besides the kids who asked me for answers during group assignments.

My mother's silver car sat alone in the driveway as I walked towards my house, hands shoved deep in my sweatshirt. A gloomy light greeted me as I entered, kicking my shoes off, just to the right of the door, making my way into the living room where I deposited my backpack on the couch. A single light was on; the rest of the house was dark. My phone read 5:30- guess I was making my own dinner. Dad probably wouldn't be home till seven. Snorting softly, I made for the stairs, padding up them, sliding down the hall in my stockinged feet to stop before my parents' bedroom. Rapping softly against the door I leaned my head in close to listen.

Not a sound reached my ears. I knocked again, this time a little louder. Nothing. Sighing deeply, I turned and made my way back downstairs. If she was asleep, I wasn't going to wake her.

Wandering into the kitchen, I yanked open the fridge and gave it a once-over. Chicken salad, a few yogurts, leftover meatloaf and cold cuts. I closed the fridge with a sweeping motion of exasperation and reached for the freezer. Bagel bites, pizza bites, pizza, and one lone potpie were the only things that appealed to me. I was in no mood to cook. For a moment I was lost, the freezer faded out of focus, and I just stood there.

Gah, come on. I shook my head and swept the door shut. Yogurt it was. Lemon. What a joy. Sitting down at the table, I pulled out my phone, tucking one leg up onto the chair with the rest of me, spoon in one hand, the other hovering over the phone screen. There were three texts from Abby waiting for me and two from Jamie.

You ask your parents yet?
My mom wants to know.
How was school?

I never did quite understand how Abby went through the whole day without texting me until she got home. It had been different before, but we were closer then, it had been months since I'd seen her. Why couldn't she just come here?

Dad's not home; mom's still asleep. School sucked. Couldn't get myself to talk to anybody.
Could you come here, maybe??

Thumb flying, I moved on to Jamie's texts.

The sound of a car pulling into the driveway distracted me. Glancing up and to my right, I gazed through the living room and out the front window just in time to see my dad exit his car and make his way towards the front door. My stomach churned ever so slightly. I stood up quickly, tucking my phone into my back pocket, snatching up the half-eaten yogurt and throwing it in the kitchen trash as I passed through. I moved quickly down the hall that connected the kitchen to the front entrance and darted into the living room. Snatching up my backpack I made for the stairs, knowing I would meet him at the door, keeping my head down. The door opened when I was on the third step, and I did not stop.

If he noticed me, he didn't say anything. The door closed as I turned the corner at the top of the stairs, and I could hear him walking into the living room before I closed the door to my room behind me. I could hear nothing but the tremoring of my heart. After a while, he would come up to see me, but the extra half hour to an hour of quiet would be welcome. Didn't he get that I didn't want to talk to him?

Letting my backpack fall to the floor, I made for the bed, pulling my phone back out as I went. In the back of my mind, I could feel the tiredness start. The thought of homework flashed through my mind as I answered Jamie's texts. She was having a rough day and wanted to talk about it. Which was fine, I supposed, meant that I'd have to wait to talk to her about my day though. A sigh left my lips as I unzipped my backpack, pulling out my laptop and an assortment of school books.

I don't really want to come over to ur place. Ur parents always make everything so weird.

I gazed at Abby's response with a pang of irritation.

She wasn't wrong, but at least my parents didn't fight in front of her. And she hadn't even mentioned anything about my bad day. What the hell was that about? Why had she asked, if she wasn't going to actually talk to me about it?

Fine, I have to wait until my mom wakes up though, I don't want to talk to my dad, he'd probably just say no anyway.

I tossed my phone a little away from me, flexing my fingers in frustration. Another sigh, deep and full of exasperation, escaped my chest, leaving behind the faint dull hints of pressure that threatened to turn into little pricks of pain. Gazing down at the clutter of notebooks that surrounded me and the password screen of my laptop, I found no motivation within myself. Instead, I became acquainted with a hollow sort of restlessness that started in my chest and moved immediately to my brain, making me want to do anything else and nothing else all at once. I heard my phone vibrate but didn't look at it.

Come on, Cathy, get going. You've got work to do, come on.

The words seemed to get eaten up by the little void as I angrily typed my password. Reaching out for my phone, I picked it up, spinning it around in my fingers for a few moments. Feeling it vibrate again, I set it back down. I wanted to get some work done before he came up to talk to me, or worse, woke mom up.

I heard him on the stairs first, and my heart contracted. He didn't knock, never did, walking across the threshold arms held awkwardly at his side, bent at the elbow and outstretched as if he was going to shake the hand of some invisible man.

"Hi, Cathy, how are you today?"

His voice was bright even if the words sounded extremely formal, like a CEO welcoming some other important businessman. There was a faint rushing sound in my ears as my heart quickened. Removing my earbuds, I smiled at him.

"Hey."

"How was school?"

He stood awkwardly in the middle of the room, feeling the tension and not knowing what to do with it. I felt bad.

"Eh, it was okay."

My eyes flicked from him to the work scattered around me, as I inched my hand closer to the upside-down phone that lay just out of reach. It felt as if I was suffocating. Every time my eyes met his, I could feel the tension slide down my spine.

"Lot of homework?"

"Not really."

"You want anything for dinner?"

I shrugged.

"I already ate."

"Oh," he seemed disappointed. "Well, if you get hungry, let me know, I'll make you something."

"Thanks."

I turned away from him then, gazing down at the math problem I'd written out, thinking about it but not really.

"Well, I'll leave you to it then."

He was definitely disappointed, and I felt bad, but I didn't want to spend time with him, his food never tasted normal anyway. Besides, every time I looked at him all I could hear was the noise, and all I could feel was muted terror. He didn't close the door behind him, and I couldn't bear to call after him. That could wake mom up. Pushing aside all of my notebooks, laptop, and clutching my phone; I walked to the door and closed it silently.

Six texts were waiting for me. I didn't want to answer any of them. Climbing back into bed, I wrapped a blanket around me, put my headphones back in and stared vacantly down at my homework.

Noise from my mom's room broke through the silence between songs and jolted me into cognition. Sitting up groggily I looked down at my phone. Twelve. Twelve text messages from only two people. Ten of them were from Jamie. I sighed. People needed to learn to wait. Jamie was still having a rough day, and now she was upset that I'd been ignoring her. Geeze, it hadn't been that long, had it? Only like an hour? Two hours...oops. I sent a quick text to Abby and then started typing my long response to Jamie's claims of being ignored and not mattering to me at all. It wasn't like she ever took the time to listen to me rant about my life.

A soft knock reached my ears. I looked up as mom poked her head into the room, standing tentatively in the doorway. She looked half asleep still.

"Hey sweetie, I didn't know you where home. You hungry? Want me to make you something?"

I thought about it. I was hungry. But if I went downstairs, I'd have to be with both of them, and that didn't appeal to me in the slightest. Besides, I still had a bunch of homework to do, but if I didn't then, I wouldn't get to spend any time with mom before she went to work. What the hell kind of options were those? I took a deep breath.

"Yeah, sure, I'll be down in a minute."

"Okay," my mom flashed me a tired smile and disappeared down the hall.

My phone buzzed three times.

Jamie.

The girl was impossible.

Disengaging from the mass of blankets, I stood up. Gazing down, I was faintly aware of my rumpled sweater, full bladder, dry lips and tired eyes. You're a real looker Cathy.

Trudging down the hall to the bathroom, I listened intently for any voices downstairs. The faint murmur of voices was all I could hear. That was good. Better both than silence or any of the other louder and more terrifying alternatives.

Making my way downstairs, I saw my dad sitting on the couch absorbed in his tablet, a notepad next to him covered in scribbles and little diagrams. I didn't say anything to him. Bypassing the room altogether I walked down the hall into the kitchen where my mom stood in front of the fridge, her mouth twisted in concentration, her thin body dressed in sweats and an old yellow shirt.

"Not a lot of options tonight. You want anything specific?"
She switched from fridge to freezer.

I did. Sausage and rice to be specific, which we had the ingredients for, but I had been too lazy to make for myself. Opening my mouth, I said

"Not really, whatever's easiest."

The look my mom gave me was one I couldn't meet with my eyes, so I flashed her a smile and turned to hop up onto the countertop.

"How about pizza then?"
"That sounds good, need help with anything?"
"No, that's okay, that's what the microwave is for."

Pulling the box out of the freezer, she set about getting it ready. A quick glance at the sink told me what my dad had made for himself, a sandwich. How original.

"You want to do anything while the pizza cooks? Play a card game or something?" my mom moved her hands about as she spoke.

I shrugged. It could give us something to do at least. I wish dad would go upstairs or something; it always felt odd to sit and play while he was off in the other room as if we didn't exist at all. But what the hell, we could still have fun, right? Right? Better than nothing. Right?

"Go fish?" I prompted

"Sure," mom flashed me a big smile and walked into the living room, returning with a deck of cards. "I'll deal first.

The microwave went off, and my dad seemed to snap out of his trance and look around. Shaking his head, he got up and went upstairs, his eyes never leaving the tablet screen. I sighed. My muscles tensed, ready to push me up so I could get the food, but mom was one step ahead, rising quickly from her chair and rushing over to the microwave, pulling the plate out and dashing back over to me with a smile on her face.

"We've got time for a few more rounds."

Sliding back into her chair, she began to deal out cards.

The first bite of pizza brought a feeling of heaviness as I glanced at the clock. 7:45. Fifteen minutes and then she'd be gone, and I'd be alone. The anticipation was like a weighted blanket that I could feel wrapping its way around me.

"Got any sevens?"

We played cards. It's what we did.

It gave the muted swirl of emotions that rattled around my chest a warmth that I found distinctly confusing and caused my body to shiver. As if it were all real and not just in my head.

It was time. 8:00.

The cards got packed up. Mom put on her coat, grabbed her purse and pulled her shoes on one by one. Just like every other night. Holding out her arms, she pulled me in, kissing my cheek and hugging me tightly.

"Don't stay up too late, okay? I'll see you in the morning. I love you."

"No promises. Love you too."

I held on to her for an extended moment, but knowing she had to leave, I pulled away and flashed her a smile.

She gave me that look again.

Wrapping her hand around the doorknob, she yelled up the stairs.

"George, I'm heading out!"

I could hear him moving around upstairs, then his footsteps coming down the hallway until his whole form appeared.

"Okay, have a good night."

There was an awkward pause. With a wave to him and a smile to me, mom pulled open the door and walked out. I followed just behind her, taking hold of the door and closing it for her. Moving back into the living room, I watched her walk down the little walkway, get into her car, and go through her normal routine. Purse in the passenger seat, music, and gloves on. Then she backed up, swinging out into the street and drove off. Faintly I heard dad walk back to their room.

Me? I stayed at the window for a while, curling up into the couch staring out into the darkness of the neighborhood, wanting to think about something but not really thinking about anything.

Homework.

I still had some of that to do, didn't I?

I reached into my back pocket and pulled out my phone.

There were a lot of texts, all from Jamie, well, mostly from Jamie.

Taking a deep breath, I thumbed away my lock screen and made for the stairs.

The night blurred around me in a haze. Abby was impossible, as always. I'd forgotten to ask my mom about going to visit her, and she wasn't happy about it. Jamie wasn't faring much better. It seemed my attempts to console her had only succeeded in making her day even worse.

Way to go, Cathy.

Tossing my phone aside with a sigh of agitation, I packed up my books, changed into PJ's, turned out all the lights and wrapped myself back up in blankets. Closing my eyes, I waited for sleep to overtake me.

L̲ight flooded my eyes.

A moment of panic flooded me, as I realized that I couldn't hear my alarm. Scrambling out of bed, I looked around frantically for my phone. I found it between my bed and the wall. The time was 5:30. I muttered a curse and was about to climb back beneath the covers when I heard it, escalating over the sound of my racing heart. Voices, coming up through the heating vent that was on the other side of my room, making anything from downstairs sound as if it were in my room.

Oh no.

My heart started beating even faster, but now my hearing seemed to have become pinpoint and enhanced. I stood, unable to move, listening to the voices from downstairs.

"I don't understand why you can't just do it, George."

"Because I have work to do, important work. I don't have time to go grocery shopping."

"Come on, it's an hour and a half of your time, two at the most. You can't take two hours of your life to go shopping for your family?"

There was a moment of silence where all I could hear was the beating and rushing of my heart.

"I don't know what to buy; it'll be easier if you go."

"What about me, George? What about the work I have to do? The work that makes us money?"

"What are you saying, Claire? My writing has made us plenty of money; you don't have to make me feel worthless just because you're upset."

"You know what, forget about it, I'll go this morning after I finish off the reports."

"Alright, if that's really what you want."

Everything fell into silence, and finally, I was able to move, crawling back into bed and pulling the blankets up over me, curling up into a ball. That hadn't been so bad, in the end, they'd had worse, right? Right. Much worse. At least no one had thrown anything this time. That was a plus. After what felt like forever but was only a few minutes, I heard the front door open, then close, followed by the sound of a car door doing the same. It was only 5:45. I had fifteen more minutes and absolutely no motivation. Going shopping with my mom sounded way better than sitting in school all day. She was probably crying though…I hated it when she cried.

It was going to be one hell of a day.

December 9th, 2016

3:30 A.M.

What is this?

I'm cold, but I'm not cold.

Sad, but definitely not...everything was echoing, silently, of course, filling my mind with a vastness that wrapped itself around me. My whole body twitched suddenly, and I sat up in bed, putting my right palm up against my temple.

Ow.

The word echoed in the silence of my room echoing along, matching the pulsing ache that seemed to emanate from my chest. I tried to think, to speak, but found myself incapable. It was strange, and more than terrifying. All involuntary action had suddenly been handed over to me. I had to make myself breathe because I kept holding my breath.

Then, a thought.

Useless.

That's right; you're useless.

You know it.

Your friends did too, that's why they won't talk to you anymore.

Mom and dad definitely know it, they created a useless child.

It's why your grades are bad, useless B's and C's that will never amount to anything.

What is this?

There's pain, like when you stub your toe or break your arm playing sports or being just plain stupid. Those are easy, they have a clear beginning, and generally, they have a clear ending, too. Not this.

I couldn't figure out where it had come from or why it hurt so much, weighing down and tightening around me. Feeling produced thought, and since the thoughts were mine, I agreed with them. So when I heard my own mind say, in my own voice...

You're useless.

You're going to fail that test tomorrow.

When it remembered the catcalls and jeers of others, not in their voices but in mine.

You're ugly.
You're stupid.
Come on Cathy, pay attention.
Cathy cuts herself at night.
Cathy, why don't you just kill yourself, not like anyone's going to miss you.
I believed the words because they were mine. How could I ever be wrong about myself?

I blinked awake, and everything hurt.
My chest. My eyes. My head.
The alarm was blaring. 6:00 A.M.
Walking down the hall, I could hear the faint sound of snoring coming from my parent's room; mom was asleep. A quick listen at the top of the stairs told me no one was there. Looks like I'll be making my own lunch today. I stood in the bathroom for several minutes, staring at the shower, completely undecided.
I ended up in my bed, staring up at my phone, scrolling through Tumblr, waiting for the seconds to tick by. Knowing I should shower, get dressed and pack a lunch but feeling certain that I would do none of those things. Well, I would get dressed, that was a given, but the rest of it, no. With ten minutes to spare I threw off my PJ's, replaced them with real clothes, grabbed my backpack off my bedroom floor and headed for the bus stop.
As I walked, a voice whispered in my mind.
You're going to fail this test Cathy; you didn't study.
Maybe it'll be fine.
Maybe…

I failed the test.
Of that I was certain.
I packed the pain away and pushed through the day, struggling to keep my mind focused. The moment I was home, curled up on the couch, forcing myself to eat a hot pocket because I was starving and couldn't take it anymore, the tears came in a flood.
Useless.
Lazy.
Sack of shit.

I wanted to go upstairs and wake my mom up, crawl into bed next to her and just cry…but she needed to sleep, that was more important, and dad, he wouldn't understand. He'd just tell me that I should have studied, worked a little harder, or he'd just ignore me completely and say something like, "well that's just too bad."

One day maybe I'd figure which one I hated more.

Suddenly I wasn't hungry.

Wandering over to the kitchen trash I let the half-eaten Hot Pocket fall away. Wiping my eyes, I circled around, grabbed my backpack, and headed for my room. There was homework to do. Maybe if I texted Abby, she would text me back. Someone had to talk to me, right? That's what friends were for…

You don't have friends Cathy.

Not anymore.

No, that couldn't be right. Maybe they were just busy and didn't have time…

Come on, Cathy; it takes like thirty seconds to send a text message; just face it, they don't want to talk to you. And when they do, they just want something from you.

They just want to talk about their day, I listen to them, and they listen to me…friendship…right.

I was gripping a pencil tightly in my hand, sitting cross-legged on my bed, staring down blankly at what was supposed to be my math homework. The impulse to break the pencil shot through me in a fit of frustration, and I let it drop.

What was that?

That was new.

Heaving a sigh, I fell backward, at an angle, wrapping my arms around my shoulders as a queasy feeling sprouted in my stomach, spreading up to my chest.

Deal with it, Cathy; you don't want to fail your assignments like you did that test.

Let's go. Let's go, Cathy. Let's go.

Forcing myself upright I found my pencil, turned my eyes to the assignment and went to work. Turning my focus away from the pain in my chest, it faded away, but somewhere in the back of my mind, I knew. It would be back.

And part of me was happy about it.

The more I felt my chest ache, the louder the silence seemed to be until the very air itself seemed to be oppressive. Waiting to fall asleep, to get tired, forgetting that I was already exhausted but just couldn't stop my mind from churning.

Churning…but empty still…come on, Cathy, which is it?

And why are you even still awake? You should have been asleep hours ago; it's three A.M. This is why you fail tests.

Hurts too much to sleep.

I whispered the words aloud, breaking the silence. It made my body quiver as if it was afraid of my voice.

The silence had moved to my body. That feeling you get when your foot falls asleep? It had wrapped itself around me causing my breath to come in strange, uneven intervals, loud and ragged.

Hearing it made me agitated.

Then the echoes started.

A thought.

Memories, all playing at once.

Yelling, crying, the sound of doors slamming, car engines revving, voices apologizing, shoulders shaking, chairs scraping, footsteps stomping, someone laughing, is that a smile? No, no it's a face full of tears, mom's face, mom's tears, no, dad's face, dad's tears, no, no, no, my face, my tears. Mine!

I could feel it all.

The emotion crashed and pulsed around me. Then it mixed together, swirling, and I didn't know what was what.

A smile. Sadness, no, that was wrong. A frown, a laughing frown, no, no, that wasn't right either. Door slams, happy? No!

With a silent scream, my body swung, even scrambled, upright, my palms rising up to crash against my head.

One, two.

One, two.

One. Two. Three.

Halfway through another swing at my temple, my hands finally stopped, and I sat, breathing heavily, shaking. For a moment, perhaps a little longer, I was frozen then all the energy left me, and all that remained was a total exhaustion that covered every bit of me. Sinking back into my bed I closed my eyes…

There was sunlight in my window.

February 3rd, 2016

1:45 A.M.

Their last fight reverberated inside my head, sending shivers through my whole body.

I couldn't hear what they were saying, only see their faces. Feel the emotion that had swept through me then course through me now.

Get it together, Cathy. Just calm down, breath, breath, come on, they always yell, it's not your fault.

Then why were they fighting about me?

I coughed. Or was it a choke…was I wheezing? Whatever it was made my chest ache.

They're upset you're doing so poorly in school, if you were a better student, this wouldn't have happened. Mom wouldn't be sleeping on the couch, she needs her rest, she has to work, if she's tired tomorrow, that's on you. What if she's too tired to drive and gets in an accident, that's on you too.

Everything seemed to rush all at once as agitation exploded outward from my head, sending adrenaline through my body. A scream swelled behind my closed lips. I forced it back, swallowing the noise, body tensing, lungs locking. A few second later I let loose a breath I hadn't even realized I'd been holding.

The air around me seemed to have become heavy, pressing on me. The scream I'd swallowed had found its way into my mind so that I could hear it.

It was, so loud.

My fists were pounding against my temple.

Pain spurted across my forehead, cutting through oppressive air, sending a shock wave through my body, purging it.

The air mutated back to itself, no longer heavy but light and cool. In an instant my chest was still, my mind was clear. All that was left of the moment was the ragged sound of my exhausted breathing.

Fumbling for my phone, I thumbed it on.

2:00 A.M

Four hours…it wasn't going to be enough.

It wasn't ever enough.

"What do you want from me, George? We don't make enough for you to try this. Why can't you understand that?"

Mom's voice jolted me awake as it echoed up through the heating vents from the first floor. It only took an instant for my heart to catapult into a panic. My whole body started to shake as my ears started to ring with memories of their last fight, while a mental haze wrapped itself around my brain. A well of emotion balled up inside my chest and catapulted up to my head so that I buzzed with anger and exhaustion.

The sound of feet slamming downstairs registered faintly in the back of my mind as the hum of angry voices grew louder. I couldn't remember leaving my room, but I must have because I was now halfway from the foot of the stairs down the little hallway that connected our front entrance to the kitchen.

"Shut up!"

Someone was screaming. I couldn't see through the haze of panic and rushing blood. Everything looked distorted, like the whole world was pulsing, the shocked look of my parents' faces somehow the center of my vision, larger than anything else around me.

"Shut up!"

The loudness of my own voice seemed to cut through the haze, and I was suddenly painfully aware of how tense my body was, how tightly my fists were clenched, how wet my cheeks were with tears.

"Cathy, Cathy you need to calm down, everything's fine, Cathy!"

The world snapped back to normal for a second at the sound of mom's voice, and I wondered faintly how long I'd been yelling.

I paused for a breath and couldn't hold my body so tightly anymore. My shoulders sagged as my arms wrapped themselves around themselves as a tremor ran down the length of my body. Just to the right dad was staring at me, wide-eyed, his hands shaking ever so slightly.

Mom reached for me, and I didn't resist her.

"Honey, it's okay, we were just talking, there's nothing to worry about, it's okay."

Then why are you sleeping on the couch?

The thought flashed through my mind, turning the warm embrace I was now trapped in a little colder.

What the hell, Cathy, look at what you did, you scared them. Now they've got that to argue about, too. First, you alienate all your friends, then you go and make your parents hate you, too? Way to be, Cathy. Way to be.

"Why don't you go get dressed, and I'll get your lunch ready for you? George, we can finish this conversation later."

"Right…I'll give you a hand."

I headed for the stairs.

Why do my legs feel so heavy?

Now I just hurt all over. Remember to get aspirin, or something before you go.

Good lord, you look terrible!

Get yourself together Cathy, come on.

What the hell did you even just do anyway?

The porcelain of the sink felt cold in my hands as I leaned over, staring into my own red and puffy eyes.

They're going to think you're crazy.

Maybe it'll snap them out of it, and they'll actually get along for once?

Hah.

Just keep calm for a while, and hopefully, they'll just let it go, besides, what are they gonna do about it anyway?

The lunchroom was loud, and I was alone.

Come on Cathy, just find a familiar face and ask if you can sit.

They ignore you; they can't hate you if they don't pick on you.

But if they ignore me, they obviously don't like me, if they liked me they would say something.

Didn't that girl Susan invite me to sit with them the first day, maybe I can sit with her?

No, no, that wouldn't work, I turned her down, and she never asked me again, and she doesn't even look at me when I see her in class.

I guess she was offended that I didn't want to sit with them.

What about...
"Excuse me?"
"What?"

Who is...I don't know him. Have I seen him before? No, he's cute, I'd have remembered. I'm good with faces.

"Hi, I'm John. What's your name?"

John...definitely don't know a John...what could he possibly want? No one ever talks to me; it's why I always sit here. Oh, I'm supposed to say something, right? He's giving me a weird look, or maybe it's just a look, come on Cathy, say something.

"Oh. Hi. I'm Cathy."

Smile at him or something. Don't make yourself look like a total freak.

"Nice to meet you. Do you mind if I sit here? Today's my first day, and I don't know anybody."

Why is my heart beating so fast? Geez, Cathy, calm down. Just because he's the first person to talk to you in the past four months...stop staring and say something!

"Uh, sure, yeah, I don't mind."

"You sure?"

Why'd you have to make it weird?

"Yeah," I gave him what I hoped was a convincing smile.

"Okay, cool," he sat down.

Watching him unpack his lunch I couldn't help but wonder, what kind of person he was, this...John.

My mom was waiting for me when I got home.

Why wasn't she asleep? She needed rest. Damn it, Cathy, if you hadn't freaked out this morning she would be asleep right now instead of about to ask you a million questions and be tired for the rest of the day.

"Hey, sweetie, you doing okay?"

She was fidgeting with her fingers, her whole body tense as if she thought I was going to explode.

"Yeah, fine. Sorry about this morning."

As if it was my fault. Come on, don't be rude, she doesn't deserve that, it's not her fault, either.

"It's okay," mom sighed heavily, "I understand. I'm sorry about the yelling."

I nodded. Feeling tears well up in my eyes, I gave her a hug.

"You should get some sleep, mom; don't you have work?" I spoke through the hug, my words muffled.

"Actually, I have an interview I have to get to first. You going to be okay by yourself? I can see if..."

My heart skipped a beat.

"No, I'll be fine, just tired. Good luck with your interview."

I gave her a smile.

Why hadn't she told me about that sooner...did she not want people to know about it? Where was she interviewing? Would we have more money? That would be nice; maybe they wouldn't fight as much then.

Trudging up the stairs to my room I left my backpack fall to the floor.

You need to get school work done, Cathy.

The thoughts got lost in a haze of tiredness that pressed against my whole head. Not bothering to change I crawled underneath the covers and...

February 18th 2016

I woke to an eerie quietness.

Today's the day, Cathy. You gotta get up, go to school, and do something fun. Maybe Abby wouldn't be busy for once.

Yeah, sure.

Can't hurt to try though...

Pulling back the curtains I peered outside, taking in the sun covered neighborhood and the big tree that sat outside my window.

Weird. Where's dad's car? He's never up this early.

I fumbled for my phone.

6:00 A.M.

Normally he's still asleep.

Eh, whatever, means I don't have to talk to him.

The floor creaked softly beneath my feet as I walked down the hall to the bathroom.

What was that?

I stopped at the top of the stairs, hand on the knob of the bathroom door, listening.

Oh no.

No.no.no.

I was standing in the living room. Head rushing. Heart aching.

"Mom?"

She looked up at me startled as if she hadn't heard me approach.

"Mom, what happened?"

But I saw the wedding ring in her hand, and I knew.

My whole body started to shake.

Fucking, piece of shit, bastard, what the hell.

She reached out for me then, and I sort of fell into her arms.

The echoes started in again. My skin crawled with numbness while my mind raged.

How could he do this?

Didn't even say anything...give a warning?

Or was it always this bad and I didn't know? What the hell.

It wasn't all that bad...was it?

We had fun, sometimes, right?

Trips to the movies.

That hike up in New York...board games?
Right?
...why didn't someone tell me?
I could have prepared for this.
Wait. What are we going to do now?
How are we...what...I don't.
I'm going to be all alone...mom has to work and he's not here...
It's nice to know someone's here, even if I haven't...
Does my heart hurt because I miss him or because I don't miss him at all?
Fucking bastard.

I can't remember the rest of the day. It passed by in a haze that felt heavy, pressing against my body from every angle as I walked from one class to the next, not saying a word, fighting back the impulse to scream at everyone and everything.
"Hey, are you okay?"
"What? ...oh. Yeah."
Don't make it weird, Cathy. You only have a few more hours left. You can do this. No one has to know.
"Okay, you just look sad today."
See, maybe you should tell him. He's been nothing but nice since you met him.
"Just tired."
"Oh, yeah, okay I get that. Hey, have you seen...?"

I was home, lying in my bed, my body too heavy to do anything.
Everything's fine.
Yeah, sure.
Maybe he just couldn't take it anymore, take me anymore, I did freak out at him.
You freaked out at mom too, but she didn't walk out.
He's just stupid.
Not like we ever got along anyway.
Then why's it hurt so much?

Because he's my dad…I guess, never really felt much like one.

Why'd they even get married in the first place?
Come on Cathy, get over it.
You knew this was gonna happen.
I should text Abby…let her know…
Why bother? She's not going to answer anyway.
Everyone leaves…maybe there's something wrong with me…do they hate me?
Do I hate me?

May 13th 2016

2:45 A.M

The echoes of emptiness pressed against me.
My chest ached. The whole room seemed to be ringing. The pain from my chest latticed out, arching down to my stomach, causing me to curl up into a ball. Everything felt heavy. Every now and then I could feel myself take a breath as if I had suddenly remembered that I needed air.

Look at you. You're barely going to pass your classes.

Your best friend told you she didn't want to talk to you again after only having talked to you at all for like a week.

What the hell is wrong with you. You make everyone leave.

Pretty soon you're gonna say the wrong thing to John, and he's gonna leave, too.

If dad hadn't already left, mom probably would have.

And she's probably just pretending.

What do you even do anyway?

Do poorly at school.

Spend hours and hours on the internet reading about people who are way better than you.

You add so much to the world, Cathy.

Gained weight too.

John probably hates that he has to sit at the table with a fat girl.

He's always nice to me though.

That's because he feels sorry for you.

He doesn't actually like you.

Maybe I shouldn't sit with him then…

No, why bother, one more month and then I won't see him for the whole summer, and he'll forget about me.

It's been three months since dad left and he hasn't asked to see you once.

Why are you even here?

I didn't ask to be here.

I was out of bed and pacing.

One. Two. Three. Four. Turn.

One. Two. Three. Four. Turn.

The finger on my right hand kept running through my hair, around my neck, across my face and then down my left arm. My breaths kept getting held behind tight lips until my lungs would ache and I would let all the air, hissing, out.

Failure.

Waste of space.

Ugly.

Stupid.

Mean.

Pudgy little freak.

GAH!

Shut up.

Shut up.

SHUT THE FUCK UP.

The base of both my palms flew to either side of my forehead and pressed down hard. My legs gave out in a strange, slow way. As if I really meant to fall but was resisting the urge all the same. I landed on my side, curled up, squeezing my head, trying to command my mind to top.

You drive everyone away.

No one wants to be near you.

Mom has too. It would be illegal for her just to leave you alone.

There has to be at least one.

That's why dad left.

Because he could.

You fat idiot.

You're useless.

No good to anybody.

I lay back against the bed, wrapping my arms around my legs, pulling them up against my chest.

"It's not true. Abby just lives too far, and I've been ignoring her."

She could have reached out to you.

"I told her I'd text her though, and I never did."

So? If she were really your friend, she would have talked to you regardless.

"Maybe she just felt like I was being mean. That's what she said the other day…"

You were the one going through a move and a divorce. If she can't handle that, then good riddance.

My head was pounding against my knees. The pain in my chest had moved up into my throat and head. Everything echoed. The whole world sounded like it was humming.

John's going to leave for the summer and forget about you. He hasn't even asked for your number.

"I don't think he has a phone."

This is 2016, of course he has a phone.

"No, didn't he say his parents wouldn't let him get one until next year? And he doesn't use the same social media as me…"

He probably made that up so that he doesn't have to talk outside of school.

"Why would he be so nice if he didn't like me…he doesn't have any other friends, either."

That you know of.

I was on my feet. Screaming. No sound came out of my mouth, but I was screaming all the same.

One. Two. Three. One. Two. Three.

My right hand smashed against my skull as I tried to jar myself out of the echoing hollowness.

It didn't work.

It had always worked before.

Shit.

My whole body shook, arms stiff at my side, the room screaming at me.

Then an idea floated across my mind. I'd thought about it more and more the past few weeks. I needed something stronger…something…sharper.

September 5th, 2016

I wonder where he is?

Looking this way and that, I searched for John's face in the crowd. Glancing down at my phone every couple of seconds I checked to see if he had texted me. Nothing.

Maybe he lied to you…he's probably off sitting somewhere else.

He wouldn't do that, would he? We've talked off, and on all summer, he said he'd be here.

Shifting in my seat, I winced. Last night's cut was still tender and scraping against my shorts.

Good. That's the whole point of it.

Enjoy the pain Cathy; you deserve it, after all.

"Cathy! Hey."

My head snapped around.

Finally!

Smile, be nice, and goodness, Cathy, don't do anything weird.

"Hey, John!"

I stood up awkwardly.

Should I hug him? Are we on hug basis? I haven't had a friend hug me in like a year…what if he thinks it's weird? Dang, it Cathy, sit down, you're making everything weird.

Oh, okay. I guess we're hugging. That's good.

"It's so good to see you again."

What's that even mean? We text often enough…

"Yeah, you too."

"I've got tons of stories to tell you from when I was in Michigan."

He didn't mention having any other stories…

"Well, go right ahead and start talking, you know me, I never get to do anything fun."

"You should hang with me and the crew some time, we always get around to crazy stuff. I would have invited you this summer but, you know."

Right. Michigan.

Does he really mean that though? I wonder what his friends are like in person; they sound funny whenever he talks about them.

Oh, come on Cathy, just because he likes you doesn't mean they will. They'll probably hate you, breaking up their social circle like that.

"Oh, um, maybe yeah. That sounds fun, I guess."

He gave me a look.

Why does he keep doing that??

"You okay, Cathy?" he was holding a tuna sandwich in one hand.

"Yeah, just tired."

"Sounds like someone needs a bedtime."

What am I, six?

"Oh really?" I tried to smile, raising an eyebrow at him.

He laughed.

"What? I have one, ten-thirty every night. Works like a charm."

"You don't have trouble sleeping?"

He gave me another odd look.

"Not since a year or so ago, no."

"Oh. So, what do you and your friends do anyway?"

A smile darted across his face, and he laughed.

His car was in the driveway when I got home.

Seven months he doesn't come back around, and now he shows back up without even a text or a phone call. What the fuck, man.

Walking slowly up the driveway I listened intently for any sound of an argument, or voices, but heard nothing at all. My heart slowed down, just for a second, before coming alive with panic. I couldn't hear the sound of the door opening or of my backpack hitting the floor over the rushing of my head and pounding of my heart.

Both my parents were sitting in the living room staring at me. I could see the fear in my mom's face. She knew what was brewing; she'd seen it too many times the past few months.

"Hey, Cathy."

His voice was soft, tentative, and it pissed me off even more.

"Seven months I don't hear shit from you and now."

"Cathy!"

Oh, was that out loud?

You know what, good. Why should I care?

Dad was staring at me, eyes wide.

Everything within me swelled as anger churned tightly inside my chest, rushing up my throat and out my lips.

"What are you looking at me like that for? Did you think you could just walk away and I'd be fine with it? Fuck you!"

"Cathy!"

My mom was on her feet, arms crossed, voice breaking.

"What!"

"Upstairs now. You can come back down when you're ready to act like a responsible teenager. Your father needs to talk to you about something important."

"Important? No! I don't want to talk to him."

"Cathy."

The sound of his voice made me want to throttle him. I could feel my body trembling, each nail on my fingers digging into my skin as my fists clenched.

"Shut the fuck up!"

I hate you so fucking much.

I was halfway up the stairs before I even realized I'd made the decision to move. I didn't look back at them. I didn't want to see his face.

You idiot, you're gonna make mom cry.

Well, she deserves it then, letting him back in the house. What the fuck is that about anyway? She's just as upset with him as I am.

Maybe he didn't call because she asked him not too?

No, no, she wouldn't do that, she'd talk to me.

Talk to you, did you see her face, she's scared of you!

Pull yourself together.

My hands were crashing against my head again as I paced the length of my room before twisting to the floor in a fit of frustration. I wanted to make it stop, to grab the razor blade hidden in my desk and bring myself back to reality, but I was afraid someone would walk in, so I waited. My body shaking, heart aching, mind echoing.

Eventually, dad left. I heard him go, watched the car leave from my bedroom window. Then mom came up the stairs, and instead of coming to my room to check on me she went into her own.

See. Now even she hates you.
Everyone hates you.
Dumb bitch.
I should go apologize.
No, clearly she doesn't want to see you.
Wait, maybe she thinks I don't want to see her…
No, she's the parent, it's her responsibility to check on me, besides if anything she should apologize to me…

October 4th, 2016

"Hey, you okay?"
Why does he always have to ask me that?
"Yeah, of course."
I tried to give him a reassuring smile.
"If you say so, you just seem a little off today."
Like that's any different from any other day.
"Just the usual, tired, lots of family stuff."
"Wanna talk about it?"
Like you care.
Maybe he does though…
Why do you always do this Cathy? He's been your friend for this long, you might as well tell him.
Not everything though.
He can't know about it; he'll tell somebody.
What if he could help though?
No.
I don't want anyone's help. There's nothing wrong with it; it helps, isn't that all that matters?
Hurry up and say something to him, this is getting awkward.
Damn it, Cathy, say something!
"Not really."
I forced the words out.
Damn. He looks kinda hurt, maybe I should have been a little nicer about it…
"Okay."
He flashed me a smile.

"Hey, have you ever been to a youth group before?"

A what? Youth group? No. what was that? Sounded like some after-school program for troubled kids or something.

"No, what exactly is it?"

"Oh, it's awesome. It's something my church does. Well, a lot of churches do them, but it's just a night where kids can come hang out and have fun. We play games. Hang out. All kinds of crazy stuff."

He certainly seems excited about it…

"You should come check it out. It's Wednesdays at seven at my church; I can give you the address."

"I'll have to ask my mom; I don't know if she'll be able to give me a ride."

I wonder what that would be like.

I've never been to a church before.

Doesn't really sound like church…

I don't really want to be around people, though; I'd rather just be home.

"If she can't take you, my mom probably wouldn't mind coming to get you. You really ought to come; it's fun."

What have I got to lose?

Maybe he really does like spending time with me…he invites me to everything.

Everything? Come on Cathy, you know that's a stretch.

Still…

He's tolerated me this long.

That's because he doesn't really know you.

If he knew everything about you, he'd leave.

Maybe…what if he didn't though?

What if he actually is just nice.

You thought Abby was nice, and look how that turned out.

Six years of friendship thrown down the drain because you moved further away than down the fucking street.

And what about Jamie?

All she ever did was complain all the time; she never cared about you at all.

John's not like that though; he's never asked me for anything…

Well except to hang out with him and his friends, but that's it.

"If my mom says no, I'll text you and let you know."
Come on, what are you waiting for?
Just say yes, you want to say yes, so why don't you?
Just go.

I decided I wasn't going to go.

The pitter patter of rain fighting its way through the big oak tree outside my window gave me a strange sense of calm through the aching that visited my chest every night.

Why would he ask me if he didn't actually want me to go?
What does it matter?
You've heard the stories of crazy religious people; they'll hate you just like everyone else does.
But, John's always seemed nice, wouldn't they be like him?
Of course, he seems nice; you guys don't ever talk about religion. I bet if you did, you'd find out how much he hates people, especially people like you.
People like me…what does that even mean, geez stop being so dramatic.
That's why people hate you; you can't ever calm down.
What if everyone's nice though, all religious people can't be mean, that doesn't make any sense.
Remember what Jamie used to tell you? About that Christian, she dated who was such a jerk?
Oh yeah.
John's not like that though…
How do you know, all you ever do is talk about movies and TV shows?
Twenty minutes a day plus occasionally texting isn't enough to get to know someone, Cathy, honestly.
Well, I won't go then, he'll just have to deal with it.
See, you're a failure. Can't even make good friends.
Oh god, not now.
Probably because you're so ugly and stupid.
You're mean, too. John always asks you to do stuff, and you never say yes.

Pudgy little freak. I don't know why he stays friends with me.

SHUT THE FUCK UP.

That's probably what he wants to say to you whenever you go off on some rant about one of your actor crushes.

What does he care? It's not like you're crushing on him.

And even if you did, it's not like he would want to date a mean pudgy freak like you.

You drive everyone away.

No one wants to be near you.

You keep telling him no and John won't, either.

You fat idiot.

You're useless.

No good to anybody.

I bet if you told anybody about the cutting they wouldn't even care.

Hell, I bet dad wouldn't even bat an eye.

Why don't you cut some of that fat off yourself?

What do you think repulses guys more?

The fat or all the scars you have now?

If you were stronger, you wouldn't need to cut.

But you're not.

You're weak.

Can't even control your own emotions.

My head was in my hands, fingers wound tightly around my hair, pulling it. I had sat up, my legs pulled up towards my chest, crossed at the ankles.

Shut up.

Shut up.

SHUT UP!

But I knew, it wouldn't stop.

It never stopped.

During the day it faded out, like faint white noise, but it was always there.

I needed pain to drive it away, and there was only one kind of pain that would do the job. Getting up off the bed, I pulled my fingers out of my hair and reached out for my desk drawer.

December 14th, 2016

My head was swimming.

I lay stretched out on my bed; legs crossed at the heel. My arms were extended out, left hanging off the bed, right braced against the wall.

Why did you even go?

You should have stayed home.

It was fun though…

So? How awkward was it to sit through that message? You were the only one there who had no idea what that guy was talking about.

What was all that crap anyway?

I don't even know.

I've never heard religion talked about in that way before.

It's all just a set up isn't it? An excuse for them to give us a pitch.

It was fun though…and they weren't pushy about it, at least. Maybe I'll go back next week…

It was nice to be able to laugh. John, Sebastian, and what was that girl's name…Jessica? Yeah, that's right, Jessica. They're all a lot of fun.

What if they didn't like me though?

I guess I'll have to wait for John to invite me along again, I don't want to go where I'm not wanted.

They all seemed happy though; they must have it better off than I do.

I bet they have both their parents. And I bet they don't argue all the time.

Damn, that's right, I have to go talk to that woman on Friday. Lovely.

Why does dad even want custody of me anyway? He's the one who walked away. He knows I hate him. What the fuck.

The thoughts brought memories on their tailcoats, and instantly the aching started up in my chest.

What's the point of explaining away all the pain? It was a cycle now, and I had grown used to it. So much so that I hardly even felt it anymore. Instead, I drifted away so that everything went numb, and I hardly felt conscious at all, as if I was floating in space, my body nothing but a shuddering shell of memory and emotion.

Somewhere far away I heard my phone vibrate.

Who could that be?

Reaching out I groped for my phone, fumbled it, then thumbed it on. The light from its screen blinded me for half a second.

12:30 A.M

John: (1) message.

What the heck is he doing up?

For a moment everything faded back to normal, and I could think again.

Hey, what did you think of tonight??

Don't overthink it, just be nice; you don't want to sound like a jerk.

It was okay, way different than I expected.

My chest still ached, and my head was starting to throb louder. Deep down I knew that when the conversation ended it would get worse. The inevitability scared me. It would grow until I could bear it no longer, then the blade would appear, and I'd add another scar to my body. Maybe even two, one didn't seem to be enough anymore.

March 23rd, 2017

1:45 A.M.

"But God, who is rich in mercy, because of the great love he had for us, even when we were dead in our transgressions, brought us to life with Christ (by grace you have been saved)"[1]

I had written those words down in a notebook the night before, and they had not left my head since.

Because of the great love he had for us.

He being God…right?

That's what the verse was saying, that's how Lucas had explained it anyway.

It didn't make any sense.

God wasn't real, so he couldn't love me.

But everyone I knew in that room thought he was real…

They really believe that.

What about me, though, what do I believe?

My parents never talked to me about God, or philosophy, or any of that stuff.

John believed it too, and he's not an idiot.

It doesn't make any sense. How can they believe?

It's because they're better than you.

A voice whispered in my head. It felt darker than my own, darker even than the voices that tore me apart every night.

God doesn't love you for the same reason your parents don't really love you.

You're just unlovable Cathy, accept.

Tolerable, maybe, bearable, absolutely. Loveable? Come on, what a joke. You almost never smile. You're always sad and moody, and you don't enjoy anything that's has any substance at all.

Lucas said that the Gospel is for everyone though, so why not me?

You don't even know what the word Gospel means, so don't even pretend like it applies to you.

If they knew who you really were, they would turn on you.

---

[1] Ephesians 2:4-5 (New American Bible, revised edition.)

The cutting, the filth you let go on in your head, they'd turn on you in an instant.

It doesn't matter at all if God is real or not, why the fuck should you care, he wouldn't want you.

The pain started there and so the night blurred away.

In the morning, I had three more scars living on my thighs.

"Hey, do you think God loves everybody?"

John froze, a chip halfway to his mouth, and stared at me.

"Of course I do; it says so in John 3:16. If you keep coming on Wednesday nights, you'll hear Lucas speak about it eventually."

He flashed me a smile and ate his chip, an oddly happy look in his eyes.

"oh…"

He didn't even have to think about it.

"Yeah! If you want to learn more about all of it, I'd talk to Lucas, or even read for yourself, so that you can figure out what questions to ask. He's always good about answering questions in a way that makes sense."

"Yeah…I might do that.

"I wish you would come every week; we always miss you when you're not there."

Really? That can't be right; I don't really do much when I'm there…

"I just don't always feel like being around that many people."

"I get that; I didn't always like going either. My mom made me go when I first started, and I really hated it."

"Really?"

"Yeah, it was the worst. I was really depressed and angry then but not so much anymore."

"Oh…I'm sorry, I'm glad you're doing better. What happened?"

He always seems so happy though.

"Well, you see…"

11:50 P.M.

M y phone went off, snapping me out of the numbness for just a second.

Hey, I forgot to ask you earlier. Is there anything I can pray for you about?

What the hell did that even mean?

Uh, I don't think I understand the question.

He didn't reply right away.

Great, good job, now you look like an idiot. You probably offended him. See, you're always screw things up.

Idiot!

My phone buzzed.

Oh.

You know how before the message on Wednesdays Lucas always has us bow our heads? That's prayer; it's how we can talk to God.

Well, ...that sounds absolutely crazy, I bet it never works.

You can't exactly say that to him though; then you'll really offend him.

My phone buzzed again.

Like, if you have anything you need you can ask for it...long as it isn't purely selfish, you know?"

No...not really...

Could be worth a shot though, you've got that meeting tomorrow that's gonna suck, maybe you could tell him about that.

He doesn't know about mom and dad though...

Oh, come on, you can't hide that from him forever.

Besides, he went through something similar; he's not gonna hate you just because your parents are split, his are too!

Oh...um...well my parents are getting divorced, and I have to meet with the lady whose representing me in court tomorrow, and I'm super stressed about it.

Oh, yeah, absolutely. I have to go to bed now, but you can tell me all about it tomorrow?

Sure! Goodnight!

Night!

Well, that was weird...

Damn it; now he's going to expect you to talk to him about everything

I heaved a sigh. Every second that air left my lungs, pain crept back into my body.

The next morning, I woke and four more scars had joined my thighs.

July 14th, 2017

The razor blade was in my hand and my entire body oscillating between being painfully still and quivering as if it was twenty degrees in my bedroom.
    I don't want to do this.
    Yes, you do, you deserve it, it's your punishment for driving everyone away. And for being a fat useless sack of shit.
    No one else has the guts to do it, so you have to.
    No! That's not true!
    Oh, but it is. You know it. Stop trying to deny what you already know.
    You pushed dad away.
    You made mom cry all the time, even after he was gone.
    You didn't try hard enough in school.
    You just sit around and never do anything useful.
    You who use the internet as a crutch because you're too afraid of your own damn feelings.
    You lie to your best friend every day because you're afraid to tell him the truth.
    You lie to your mom because you know you already caused her enough pain.
    You lie to your dad because you hate his fucking guts.
    No! No! NO!
    I'm different now!
    That isn't me anymore!
    It was once, but not anymore, I don't need to do this anymore!
    "God proves his love for us in that while we were still sinners Christ died for us.[2] He gave his only Son so that everyone who believes in him might not perish but might have eternal life.[3]"
    I believe!
    I believe!
    I don't need this anymore.

---

[2] Romans 5: 8 New American Bible, revised edition.
[3] John 3:16 New American Bible, revised edition.

My hands were shaking, but the rest of my body was tense and tired.

Do I really though?

The thought crept its way into my head and wouldn't leave.

I do.

I do.

I do!

The only peace I have ever felt was sitting in that large room of people listening to Lucas preach!

Or listening to John attempt to answer all my crazy questions.

I want peace!

I want all this pain to go away!

This!

I was staring at the razor blade, watching it shake before me in the dark.

It only ever makes it leave for a little while.

The pain always comes back!

I want it to stop!

"Come to me all you who labor and are burdened, and I will give you rest."[4]

I want rest!

Dear God, please!

I want it all to stop!

I couldn't tell if I was screaming the words in my head or aloud but I could feel my body moving. My legs swinging off the bed, freehand throwing my door open with a loud bang. I was down the hallway in a second and in the bathroom.

I could feel tears running down my face.

Was I crying?

It was then that I became aware of my shoulders shaking as sobs burst forth from my lips. Holding out my arm over the bathroom trash I held the razor blade in a vice grip.

Let go, Cathy.

Breathe out pain, breathe in peace.

Breathe out pain, breathe in peace.

I could hear John's voice in my head. He had told about what he used to say when he got angry to help him calm down.

---

[4] Mathew 11:28 New American Bible, revised edition.

Breathe out pain, breathe in peace, and pray.

So, I did.

Breathe out pain, breathe in peace, and pray, and mean every word of it. That's the most important part.

Dear God, help me. Give me peace.

Mean it, Cathy, you've got to mean it.

My chest felt as though it was about to explode.

I'm yours, God, please, just give me peace.

My heart broke. All the emotion drained from my body as my fingers sprang open.

The blade fell, and so did I. It landed in the trash, I on the floor, in nothing but a t-shirt and underwear, crying and shaking like a baby.

"Cathy. Cathy is that you? What's going on?"

Looking up I saw my mother standing in the bathroom doorway, dressed in her PJ's. Her eyes were tired, and she looked sad and concerned, her voice strained with emotion.

"Mom, I'm sorry. I'm so, so, sorry."

Here eye's caught sight of my thighs and her heart broke. I could see it in her eyes.

Then she was next to me, holding me, crying, whispering in my ear.

"Shhhh, it's okay sweetie. I love you; it's okay. I'm sorry too; everything's going to be okay. Shhhhh."

In that moment, wrapped in her arms, I believed her.

Something had shifted, changed. My head felt clear even though it was alight with worry. For the first time ever, I had found an especially peaceful equilibrium. With my mother's arms wrapped around me and my faith stored up tightly in my heart. The chains of pain were broken, and I was free.

July 23rd, 2017

The next Sunday my mom took me to a service at John's church. It was the same space we had youth group in every Wednesday but filled with people of all ages. We sat next to John, and his mom and the smile on his face brought one to my own.

"You ready to worship?"

What?

"What?"

He laughed.

"Sing, are you ready to sing?"

"Oh…uh, yeah, I guess."

"Good."

Up in the front of the room, men and women took up their instruments.

"I would like to invite you to rise as we turn to worship our Lord this morning."

Then as one, the entire room started to sing.

"Your love is devoted like a ring of solid gold."

the words were being projected onto a screen up on the stage for all to see and sing along.

Looking over at mom I smiled at her, giving her a quick hug.

"Like a vow that is tested like a covenant of old."

I closed my eyes and listened to the music for a moment, unsure whether or not I should sing along.

"Faithful you have been and faithful you will be

you pledge yourself to me and its why I sing."

Then a sudden joy swept through me. I was free. Free to worship, free to sing. So, I did.

"Your praise will ever be on my lips, ever be on my lips.

Your praise will ever be on my lips, ever be on my lips."

Acknowledgements

All Scripture was taken from the *New American Revised Edition* and used with the full intent to demonstrate the power of the Word of God.

The Song at the end is an excerpt from Aaron Shust's song *Ever Be*.

I want to thank my proof readers and the students of Legacy Christian Academy for contributing to this book and to the stage adaptation.

Made in the USA
Middletown, DE
25 October 2021